AMERICA FERRERA

ACTOR AND ACTIVIST

by Rachel Rose

Consultant: Mary Beltrán, Associate Professor of Radio-Television-Film, University of Texas at Austin

Minneapolis, Minnesota

Credits

Cover, 4, ©Michael Donhauser/picture alliance/Getty Images; 5, ©Nima Taradji/Polaris/Newscom; 6, ©dpa/picture-alliance/Newscom; 7, ©Andy Wong/UPI/Newscom; 8, ©Jay Yuan/Shutterstock; 10, ©Matt McClain/The Washington Post/Getty Images; 11, ©FeyginFoto/Shutterstock; 12, ©Ralf-Finn Hestoft/Corbis/Getty Images; 13, ©Albert L. Ortega/WireImage/Getty Images; 14, ©Chuck Kennedy/The White House; 15, ©Pete Souza/The White House; 16, ©Amanda Lucidon/The White House; 17, ©Mark Wilson/Getty Images; 18, ©JUSTIN TALLIS/AFP/Getty Images; 19, ©Sgt. James Hodgman/U.S. Air Force; 21, ©Bennett Raglin/ESSENCE/Getty Images; 22, ©Matt McClain/The Washington Post/Getty Images; 22, ©Jay Yuan/Shutterstock

President: Jen Jenson
Director of Product Development: Spencer Brinker
Editor: Allison Juda
Photo Research: Book Buddy Media

Library of Congress Cataloging-in-Publication Data

Names: Rose, Rachel, 1968- author.
Title: America Ferrera : actor and activist / by Rachel Rose.
Description: Minneapolis : Bearport Publishing Company, 2021. | Series: Bearport biographies | Includes bibliographical references and index.
Identifiers: LCCN 2020030862 (print) | LCCN 2020030863 (ebook) | ISBN 9781647477158 (library binding) | ISBN 9781647477233 (paperback) | ISBN 9781647477318 (ebook)
Subjects: LCSH: Ferrera, America, 1984- —Juvenile literature. | Actors—United States—Biography—Juvenile literature. | Hispanic American actors—Biography—Juvenile literature. | Human rights workers—United States—Biography—Juvenile literature.
Classification: LCC PN2287.F423 R67 2021 (print) | LCC PN2287.F423 (ebook) | DDC 791.4302/8092 [B]—dc23
LC record available at https://lccn.loc.gov/2020030862
LC ebook record available at https://lccn.loc.gov/2020030863

Copyright © 2021 Bearport Publishing Company. All rights reserved. No part of this publication may be reproduced in whole or in part, stored in any retrieval system, or transmitted in any form or by any means, electronic, mechanical, photocopying, recording, or otherwise, without written permission from the publisher.

For more information, write to Bearport Publishing, 5357 Penn Avenue South, Minneapolis, MN 55419. Printed in the United States of America.

Contents

Winner	4
Growing Up	6
Rise to Fame	10
Passion, Politics, and Human Rights	16
The Best Is Yet to Come	20
Timeline	22
Glossary	23
Index	24
Read More	24
Learn More Online	24
About the Author	24

Winner

America Ferrera made her way to the stage. Everyone in the **audience** was clapping and cheering. The 22-year-old had just won the 2007 Emmy **Award** for best actress in a **comedy** television show. America told the crowd, "It is truly an amazing, *wonderful* thing that happens when your dreams come true."

America also won a Golden Globe Award and a Screen Actors Guild Award for the same lead role in *Ugly Betty*.

America played the role of Betty Suarez.

America with her Emmy

Growing Up

America was born on April 18, 1984, in Los Angeles, California. She was the youngest of six children born to **immigrant** parents. Her mother and father had come to the United States from Honduras, in Central America. When America was seven, her father left the family. After that, America's mother raised the children by herself.

When she was a child, America liked to be called by her middle name, Georgine.

America is close to her mom *(left)*. They are both named America.

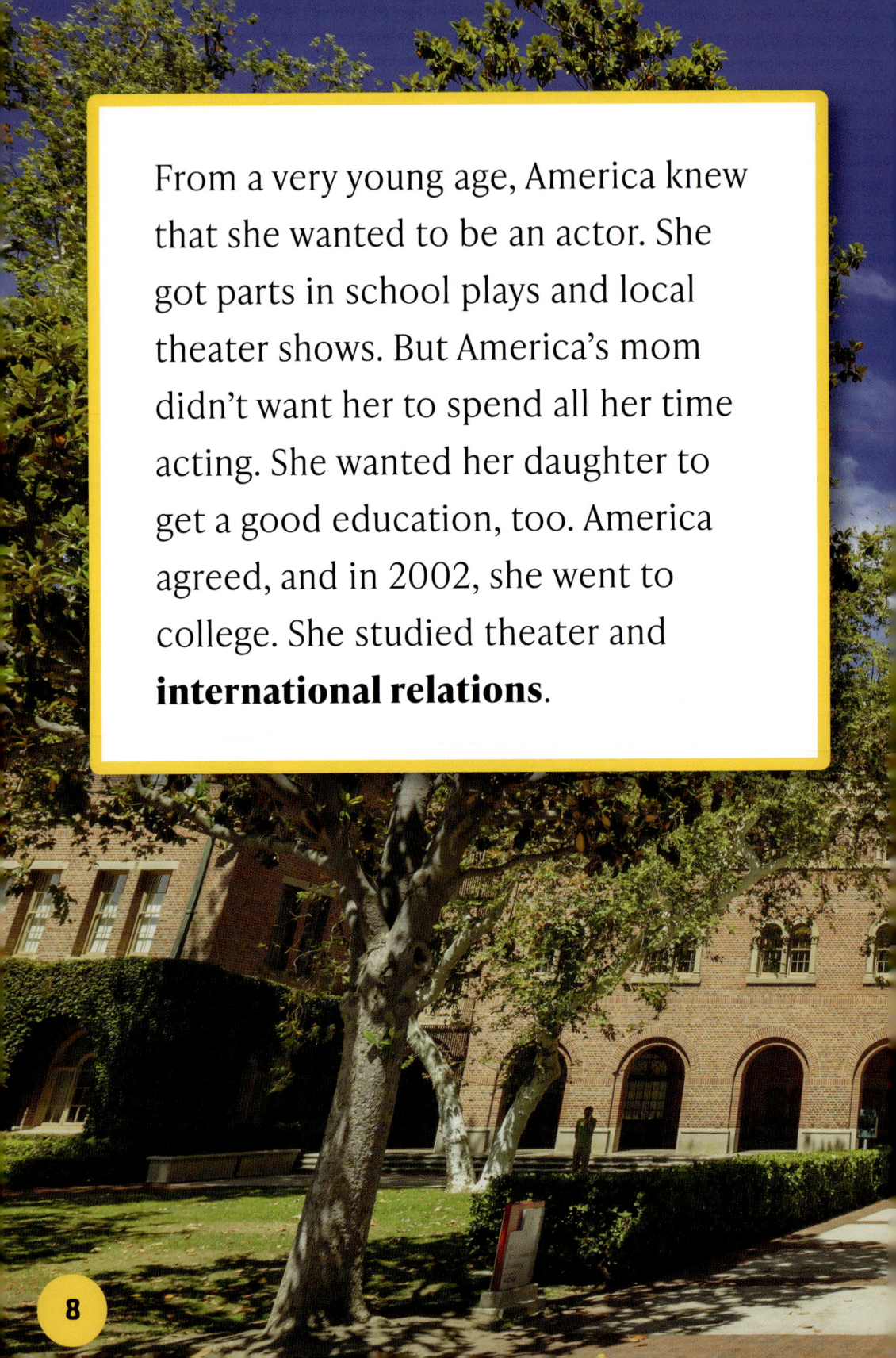

From a very young age, America knew that she wanted to be an actor. She got parts in school plays and local theater shows. But America's mom didn't want her to spend all her time acting. She wanted her daughter to get a good education, too. America agreed, and in 2002, she went to college. She studied theater and **international relations**.

America went to the University of Southern California in Los Angeles.

While she was in college, America continued to get many acting parts. Because of this, it took her 10 years to graduate!

Rise to Fame

America's acting **career** started out strong. In 2002, she got the lead role in the movie *Real Women Have Curves*. It was about the **challenges** a **Latina** girl faces living in the United States. Then, she landed an even bigger break. In 2005, she got the part of Carmen in the hit movie *The Sisterhood of the Traveling Pants*.

America (second from the left) with her costars

The Sisterhood of the Traveling Pants is about four close friends. America and her costars were great friends in real life, too!

America at the premiere of *Real Women Have Curves*

In 2006, America won the hearts of millions by playing the part of Betty in the show *Ugly Betty*. The role made her truly famous. Her character worked for a fashion magazine. While many of the people at the magazine thought she was ugly, Betty showed the value of being beautiful on the inside.

America (center) with fans

America hoped the character Betty showed Latina girls that it is okay to be themselves. America wanted to be a role model for young Latinas living in the United States.

America as Betty

The show *Ugly Betty* ended in 2010. America missed playing Betty, but she kept busy. That same year, she became the voice of Astrid, a Viking in the **animated** movie *How to Train Your Dragon*. Astrid would become a part of America's life just as Betty had. For the next decade, America played Astrid in three *How to Train Your Dragon* movies and several TV shows.

America and Ryan (right)

Just after she started training dragons, America took on another adventure. She married her college boyfriend, Ryan Piers Williams, in 2011.

14

America played Astrid (*the blonde female character on the poster*) in *How to Train Your Dragon*.

Passion, Politics, and Human Rights

Acting wasn't America's only **passion**. She became interested in human rights in college. In 2008, she teamed up with the organization Save the Children to help kids around the world. She also worked with the global organization ONE, which fights against **poverty** and sickness. Its goal is to give everybody a fair chance at living a good life.

Students at the Save the Children School in Mali, a country in Africa

America and Save the Children helped raise funds to build a school in Africa.

America also wanted to make life better for Latinos and immigrants in the United States. She joined the organization *Voto Latino* in its goal to get more Latinos to vote in the 2012 and 2016 U.S. presidential **elections**. It is important to America that Latinos have a voice in how the country is run. She stands up for the rights of immigrants and their families as often as she can.

Women's rights are important to America, too. She spoke about women and immigrant rights at the Women's March on Washington in 2017.

America encouraged everyone to vote through her work with *Voto Latino*.

The Best Is Yet to Come

America Ferrera has done many wonderful things in her life. She has acted in movies and television shows. And she has fought for human rights to make peoples' lives better. She continues to help tell new stories she feels the world needs to hear. But America still has much more to do—and the passion to get it done!

America still loves acting as much as she did when she was a child. She hopes to keep doing what she loves for the rest of her life.

One of America's recent projects took her behind the camera to make a story about Mexican Americans in California.

Timeline

Here are some key dates in America Ferrera's life.

1984 Born on April 18

2002 Stars in *Real Women Have Curves*

2005 Plays Carmen in *The Sisterhood of the Traveling Pants*

2007 Wins awards for her role in *Ugly Betty*

2012 Joins the organization *Voto Latino*

2013 Graduates from college

2017 Speaks at the Women's March on Washington

2019 Stars in *How to Train Your Dragon: The Hidden World*

Glossary

animated produced by the creation of a series of drawings or pictures that appear to move

audience a group of people listening to or looking at something

award a prize for being the best at something

career the job a person has for a long period of time

challenges problems or tasks that need extra work or effort to do

comedy a play, movie, or television show that is meant to make people laugh

elections the choosing of people for a position by voters

immigrant a person who travels from one country to live and make their home in a new one

international relations the study of world issues

Latina a woman or girl of Latin American heritage; Latino is the term used for men

passion something one cares about very deeply

poverty the state of being very poor

Index

college 8-9, 14, 16, 22
Emmy Award 4-5
Honduras 6
How to Train Your Dragon 14-15, 22
Los Angeles, California 6, 8
ONE 16
Real Women Have Curves 10-11, 22
Save the Children 16-17
Sisterhood of the Traveling Pants, The 10, 22
Ugly Betty 4, 12-14, 22
Voto Latino 18, 22
Williams, Ryan Piers 14
Women's March 18, 22

Read More

Norris, Hayley. *America Ferrera (Junior Bios)*. New York: Enslow Publishing, 2021.

Swift, Keilly. *How to Make a Better World*. New York: DK Publishing, 2020.

Learn More Online

1. Go to **www.factsurfer.com**
2. Enter "**America Ferrera**" into the search box.
3. Click on the cover of this book to see a list of websites.

About the Author

Rachel Rose is a writer who lives in San Francisco. Her favorite books to write are about people who lead inspiring lives.

24